Meg Mac...

AND

The Case of the Curious
Whale Watch

A Solve-It-Yourself Mystery

by Lucinda Landon

A BANTAM SKYLARK BOOK ®
NEW YORK · TORONTO · LONDON · SYDNEY · AUCKLAND

For Mom and Dad

"Sharks! Hammerhead sharks," said Peter. "That's what I want to see."

"It figures you'd be more interested in sharks than whales," Meg Mackintosh said to her brother, as they walked down the pier.

"This whale watch expedition is a grand idea," said Gramps. "What do whales watch, anyway?"

"*We* are going to watch *them*," said Meg, checking her binoculars. She had also brought her camera, notebook, and detective kit—just in case.

"The captain of the boat is quite famous," Gramps went on. "When he's not running whale watches, he's searching for a long-lost treasure that was buried by pirates in the 1800s, or so the story goes."

"Pirates?" said Peter.

"Lost treasure?" said Meg. "Sounds like a mystery!"

Meg, Peter, Gramps, and Skip boarded the *Albatross*.

"Welcome aboard!" boomed a hearty voice. "I'm Captain Caleb Quinn.

"That's my mate, Jasper, helping the other passengers.

"There's a Mrs. Clarissa Maxwell and her nephew, Anthony.

"And a nice old gentleman, Mr. Oliver Morley,

and a young student named Carlos de Christopher.

"That's Dr. Peck, Dr. Susan Peck, a marine biologist. I guess we're all here. OK, Jasper, cast off."

5

"Are you really searching for a lost treasure?" Meg asked the captain, as they headed out to sea.

"I have an old treasure map. I'll show it to you," the captain offered. He went up to the pilothouse and returned with the map. The other passengers gathered around.

"My great-great-uncle got it from a sailor in New Zealand many years ago; he sent it to his brother, and it was passed down through the family until it got to me. Here it is, still in the original envelope.

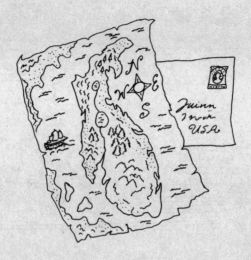

He sent this scrimshaw, too. It's a carving of a whale on a whale's tooth."

"Did you ever find the treasure?" Meg asked.

"Never did. In all these years, no one has figured out where it is. Well, on with the whale watch. I'll lock this back up. Come on, Peter, you can help me steer."

"The treasure must be worth a lot of money," said Peter, as he followed the captain up to the pilothouse.

"I'll bet it's worth millions!" said Carlos.

"I could *use* millions," said Anthony. "Don't tell Auntie, but I'm broke if my horse doesn't win at the track today."

"That map should be destroyed," Dr. Peck said to Mr. Morley. "Those treasure hunters are always digging up the environment."

"The map looked quite authentic," replied Mr. Morley. "But I doubt the captain will ever find the treasure."

"Just think," Mrs. Maxwell said wistfully, "all those gems just sitting there."

"I wish I could solve the mystery for Captain Quinn," said Meg. She noticed Mr. Morley's magnifying glass. "Are you a detective?" she asked.

"Oh, no. Not me," said Mr. Morley.

"Thar she blows!" yelled Gramps.

Gramps was right. In the distance, a whale spouted water. Then more whales came to the surface for air.

"Whales travel in groups called pods. In the spring they migrate north to cooler waters," explained the captain. He had turned off the engines and come down from the pilothouse to point out the different whales.

Meg took photographs with her instant camera and jotted in her notebook. "We're studying whales in school," she said to Anthony.

"They're just a bunch of big fish. I only came along for the ride," he replied and stretched out to sunbathe.

"Whales aren't big fish," Meg corrected him. "They're mammals."

"And they'll be extinct if we don't protect them," Dr. Peck added. "I'm researching their migratory patterns. I was just awarded a grant."

"*My* grant money might be cut," grumbled Carlos. "Then I wouldn't be able to return to college."

Mrs. Maxwell was busier filing her fingernails than watching the whales. "May I put my purse up in the pilothouse for safekeeping?" she asked the captain.

"If you like," Captain Quinn answered. "But hurry, so you don't miss anything."

In a few minutes Mrs. Maxwell returned, and seconds later the captain let out a shout. "Look! There's a finback whale!" he exclaimed. "It's one of the largest and fastest whales. They can grow to be seventy feet long and weigh as much as sixty-five tons."

Dr. Peck ran up to the pilothouse to take photos.

Peter had a telephoto lens, too. "I should get some great shots," he said to Meg. "Much better than that little instant camera of yours."

Meg ignored Peter and went over to Gramps and Mr. Morley.

"I'm hoping to retire soon," Meg overheard Mr.

Morley say. "A few investments would help."

"I hate to cut this short," said Gramps, "but I'm feeling a bit seasick. I think I'll go in the cabin and lie down."

Meanwhile, Meg noticed Jasper slipping into a lifeboat with one of Peter's comic books. "Do you help the captain hunt for the treasure?" she asked.

"Never have," Jasper answered. "But I wouldn't mind finding that treasure myself. I'd never have to get on a boat again."

Suddenly, Mrs. Maxwell shrieked, "Look how they jump in the air!"

Albatross

"That's called breaching," said Captain Quinn. "Some say the whales leap out of the water like that to try to scratch the barnacles off their skin."

Dr. Peck came down from the pilothouse, and Carlos went up to use the telescope. Then he returned to the deck to see some whales that had come quite close to the boat.

"I've already shot three rolls of film," said Peter, as he reloaded his camera. "What time is it, anyway?"

"It's exactly eleven-forty," answered Mr. Morley, flicking his pocket watch open and shut.

"Quick! On the other side!" yelled Peter, aiming his camera. "SHARK FINS!"

Everyone raced through the passenger cabin to the port side of the boat.

"It's not a shark," said Dr. Peck. "It's a humpback whale and her calf. The calf stays with the mother, feeding and learning, for about a year, during which the mother is quite protective of the calf."

"Watch! She's fluking her tail!" exclaimed Meg. "Everyone over here. Let me take your picture with the whales in the background."

"You're blocking my sun," complained Anthony, as Meg was snapping the picture.

"No, it's a storm—and it's moving in fast," said Captain Quinn, observing the clouds. "Looks like a doozy of a nor'easter. Everybody inside, it's going to get rough. And where's that mate of mine?"

Albatross

Inside the cabin, Gramps was still asleep on the bench. Captain Quinn went to the pilothouse to start up the engines. They could hear the rain begin.

"Dr. Peck is missing," worried Mrs. Maxwell. "Where is she?"

"That's not all that's missing!" said the captain, bursting back into the cabin. "My treasure map is gone! Somebody broke into the strongbox in the pilothouse and stole it. It's got to be one of you!"

The passengers looked at each other in silence. Then the cabin door blew open and in came Dr. Peck. She was drenched.

"Where were you?" said Anthony.

"*She* was in the pilothouse earlier," said Peter. "I saw her."

"I've been on the deck observing the whales," snapped Dr. Peck. "Not that it's any of your business."

"What's all the noise about?" grumbled Gramps, rubbing his eyes.

While Captain Quinn told Gramps and Dr. Peck what had happened, Meg grabbed her knapsack and darted up to the pilothouse to inspect the scene of the crime.

The padlock on the strongbox had been broken. A handkerchief and some broken pieces of metal lay nearby. Meg got out her magnifying glass to examine the clues. Then she took a photograph.

WHAT CAN YOU DEDUCE
FROM THE SCENE OF THE CRIME?

"That's Mrs. Maxwell's handkerchief," said Peter. "It's got 'CM' on it, and the captain said that her first name is Clarissa. And those are pieces of a nail file. I saw her filing her nails, too."

"Sure it's my hankie and my nail file!" cried Mrs. Maxwell. "Someone must have taken them from my purse."

"Or maybe you just wanted it to look that way," said Carlos.

"I didn't steal that old map," she answered defiantly.

"Let me examine the padlock," said Peter. "I might be able to tell if it was broken by a left-handed or right-handed person."

"Is anything else missing, Captain Quinn?" Meg asked.

"No . . . that's it," replied the captain.

"Don't worry, Captain," Peter said confidently. "I'll find that map if I have to search everywhere and everyone. I *am* the president of my Detective Club. By the way, is there any reward?"

Meg rolled her eyes. But she knew Peter was serious about solving the mystery. If I'm going to solve this, she thought to herself, I'd better do it fast—before Peter does and before we get back to shore.

"What time is it?" Meg asked Mr. Morley.

"Sorry, I don't know. My watch is jammed shut," he answered.

Meg took out her notebook and began to make a list of all the suspects and their possible motives. Before long, she realized it wouldn't be easy to spot the thief.

WHY NOT?

Just about everybody aboard the *Albatross* had a motive!

Meg was still looking over her list of suspects when Peter burst into the pilothouse. "That mate Jasper has been sneaking around all morning," he said to Meg. "I bet he had something to do with the theft."

"Jasper's had a million chances to steal the map," replied Meg. "Why would he pick today?"

"Then what about Carlos?" Peter pointed his finger accusingly. "Weren't you in the pilothouse using the captain's telescope?"

"Everything was fine when I left there," Carlos protested.

"Well, someone definitely stole my hankie and nail file from my purse," said Mrs. Maxwell, who was still clutching Anthony's hand.

"But nothing else was missing?" asked Meg. "Your wallet and all of your money are still there?"

"Yes . . . it's all there," she answered, somewhat flustered.

"What about you, Anthony?" Peter looked at him. "It's no secret that you need some cash . . . or is it?"

"Oh, no, not my little Anthony," said Mrs. Maxwell. "He'd never steal a thing."

24

"Just like that humpback protecting her calf," said Meg quietly.

"Humpback? What are you talking about?" said Mr. Morley.

"What about *you*, Meg?" Mrs. Maxwell interrupted. "You've been snooping around about that treasure map all day!"

"Meg wouldn't steal the map," Peter defended her. "She'd rather solve mysteries than cause them."

"Well, I'd be careful if I were you," warned Anthony. "Playing detective could get you into trouble."

Now I *have* to solve the case, Meg thought to herself, before I become a suspect! She thought hard. It's the timing that's important. The thief must have struck after the captain left the pilothouse and came down to point out the whales. Where was everyone after that?

Meg thought back to what had happened. She decided to draw a picture of the boat and, with the help of her photos, map out where everyone had been.

Meanwhile, the storm was getting rough. All of the passengers were huddled in the cabin, except Peter, who was timing how long it would take to run up the steps to the pilothouse, break into the strongbox, and then run back down. Captain Quinn and Jasper were busy guiding the *Albatross* through the dense fog.

"How's it going?" Gramps asked Meg, peering over her shoulder. He still looked a bit green.

"Well, it's hard to say," said Meg. "Peter thinks the nail file and handkerchief point to Mrs. Maxwell. But I doubt she would leave her tools at the scene of the crime. I think Carlos was in the pilothouse last, but it's possible someone slipped up after him. I'm still trying to figure out everyone's alibi. I also have some instant photos I took. They might show something," she confided in him.

"Let's see," said Gramps. "Nice shot of me and Skip."

Mr. Morley was sitting nearby. "I'd check out that Dr. Peck if I were you," he whispered. "She's been acting very suspiciously."

Peter overheard them and decided to get to Dr. Peck first. A wave pitched the *Albatross* sharply; Peter knocked into her and was able to dump her camera bag on the floor. The top of a lens case came off and out fell . . .

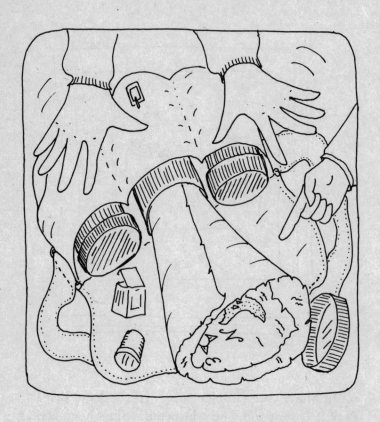

"What have we here?" said Peter triumphantly. "Looks like I've found our crook. You can forget all about your little deductions, Meg-O. The case of the missing treasure map is *closed*."

"What? How did that get there?" exclaimed Dr. Peck. "I didn't take that map. I never touched it!"

"Wait until the Detective Club hears about this," boasted Peter, as he handed the map over to Captain Quinn.

"I knew she did it," said Anthony. "Scientists are creepy."

"She said she thought treasure maps should be destroyed," said Mr. Morley. "I guess she really meant it."

"Is it the same map?" asked Carlos. "She could have copied it."

"That's my map, all right," said the captain. "I'm going to have to tell the police about this, but first we have to get through this storm."

"You're all wrong!" cried Dr. Peck. "I didn't steal the map!"

I believe her, Meg thought to herself. Something doesn't make sense. Meg looked over her drawings and photos to try to figure out what.

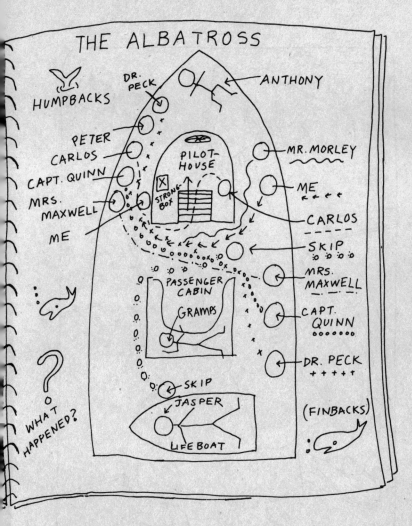

After a moment, Meg knew she was right. The case was *not* closed. Dr. Peck couldn't have stolen the map.

WHY NOT?

"Dr. Peck did go up to the pilothouse to take photographs," Meg explained to Gramps. She had pulled him out on deck, out of earshot of the others. "But Carlos went up there to use the telescope *after* she did, and he said everything was fine. Dr. Peck was on the deck with the rest of us until the storm. I remember talking to her then, and she's in the group photo I took."

"But if Dr. Peck didn't do it," said Gramps, "how did the map get in her camera bag?"

"Maybe somebody else—I don't know who—took the map and then planted it on Dr. Peck. You know, like a red herring, to throw us off the track," Meg replied.

"You mean they figured out where the treasure was and then ditched the map on Dr. Peck?" Gramps scratched his head.

"That would be pretty fast thinking," said Meg. "Four generations of Quinns haven't been able to find the treasure. But why would someone steal the map only to return it?" Meg decided to have another look at the map. She headed up to the pilothouse to talk to Captain Quinn.

"This whole thing is as foggy to me as that weather out there," said Captain Quinn, as he leaned over the steering wheel and gazed out to sea. "I don't understand why a professor of ocean life would want to steal my old map. I suspect the gold and gems are worth a tidy sum, but I've logged a lot of hours looking for that treasure—it won't come easy."

"I don't think Dr. Peck *did* steal the map," Meg said, and explained why. "Could I see the map again?"

"Help yourself," said the captain. "It's back in the strongbox."

Meg took out the map, then noticed the scrimshaw

and took it out, too. "At least the thief didn't bother with this," she said.

Meg studied the map and scrimshaw with her magnifying glass, and went over her notes and photographs again. After a while she realized that, although Peter had found the treasure map, something else was missing.

WHAT?

The envelope. They'd found the map, but not the envelope it came in. Where was it? And what difference could an old envelope make? Meg wondered.

Suddenly there was a loud CLUNK. The lights in the cabin blinked and went out. The engine was dead; the *Albatross* drifted in the storm.

"Jumping jellyfish!" yelled the captain. "Don't worry, Meg. I'll go down below and help Jasper get her going again. You stay here."

Meg could hear the other passengers scurrying about in the cabin below.

"What's happened to the power?" asked Carlos nervously.

"We're not going to sink, are we?" said Anthony.

"Are we stranded with a dangerous criminal aboard?" exclaimed Mrs. Maxwell.

"I'm not dangerous . . . and I'm not a criminal," insisted Dr. Peck. "This is absurd!"

"I found the treasure map on you," said Peter. "That's pretty strong proof."

"Where *is* the map?" asked Mr. Morley. "Someone may try to steal it again while the lights are out."

Meg clutched the map tightly, but what she was really thinking about was the envelope. In a moment, she figured out what had happpened to it—and suddenly the whole case fell into place. She ran down to the cabin.

"Listen, everybody. Dr. Peck *didn't* steal the map. I know who did!"

WHO?

"Mr. Morley!" Meg announced. "He stole the treasure map!"

"What? Not I! What would I want with a worthless old map?" asked Mr. Morley.

"Nothing," Meg agreed. "But you did want the stamp on the envelope the map was sent in. You noticed that it was very old and valuable—you even had your magnifying glass and stamp-collecting book to verify it. You waited until Captain Quinn was out of the pilothouse and everyone else was busy watching the whales, then you sneaked in and stole it. You took the treasure map to throw us off the track, and you planted it on Dr. Peck to make her look guilty. You figured that no one would ever miss the envelope or stamp."

Mr. Morley turned red as a lobster. "You have no proof. You're just playing detective," he protested. "Why, I've had no opportunity to take the map, even if I wanted to!"

"That's not true," said Meg. "You did have an opportunity."

WHEN?

"When we all ran to the port side of the boat to see the whales, you weren't there," Meg explained. "My photos prove it—you're not in the group shot. And when I mentioned that Mrs. Maxwell and Anthony were acting like a humpback whale and her calf, you didn't know what I was talking about—because you weren't there when we saw them. You were in the pilothouse stealing the map and the envelope. Anthony was sunbathing. Jasper was reading Peter's comic books in the lifeboat. Gramps was

asleep in the cabin and didn't see you. The rest of us were on deck. You took Mrs. Maxwell's nail file to break the padlock and used her handkerchief to wipe off your fingerprints. Then you rolled up the map and stuffed it into Dr. Peck's camera-lens case, which she had left on the bench in the cabin. I think you ripped the stamp off the envelope and threw the envelope overboard to be rid of it. And I think I know where you put the stamp, too."

WHERE?

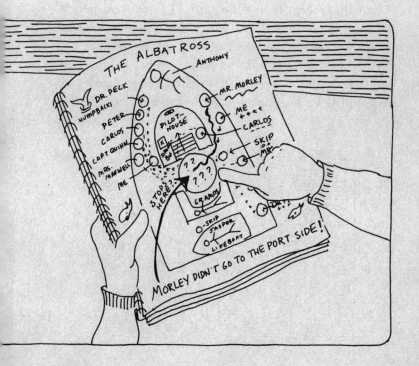

"I bet it's in your pocket watch," Meg continued. "At eleven-forty, you snapped it open and told Peter what time it was. That was before the theft. But afterward, when I asked you the time, you said your watch was jammed shut. Ten-to-one you quickly hid the stamp inside to keep it safe and dry."

"This is absolutely ridiculous," Mr. Morley insisted. "I refuse to listen to any more of these wild accusations. This amateur sleuth has clearly invented this story for her own amusement."

Captain Quinn stepped forward. "I think we'd better see your watch," he said. "If Meg's theory is as farfetched as you say, surely you won't mind if we have a look."

Peter added, "If you didn't do it, you have nothing to hide!" The others agreed. They stared at Mr. Morley as he fumbled for his pocket watch. Meg held her breath.

Mr. Morley scowled as he handed the pocket watch over to the captain.

Sure enough, the stamp was there. Just as Meg had suspected.

"I never thought you'd miss one little stamp," groaned Mr. Morley. "But such a valuable little stamp . . . an 1855 New Zealand. I can't believe I let it slip through my fingers."

"He was going to let me be arrested!" cried Dr. Peck.

There was another clunk and the engine started up. The lights flickered back on.

"I got her going again, Cap!" shouted Jasper.

"The police will take care of Mr. Morley when we get back to shore," said Captain Quinn. "It's nice to have a valuable stamp, but I'm really just happy to have my old treasure map back—even though I still don't know where the treasure is."

"But that's not all!" exclaimed Meg. "I think I can help you with that, too."

HOW?

Meg got out her magnify-
ing glass and the scrimshaw.
"If you look at the scrimshaw carefully, the whale
looks like the island on the
treasure map. And if you
turn the map this way, it re-
sembles a whale. I noticed it
when I was examining the clues.

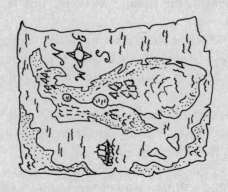

I think the sailor gave your great-great-uncle both the
map and the scrimshaw so they would complement each
other in telling the location of the treasure. So, if someone stole the map, they still couldn't figure out where
the treasure was. You need *both* of them to find it.

"See," Meg continued.
"The eye on the scrimshaw
whale looks like an 'X.' I bet
that 'X' marks the spot on
the island where you should
look for the treasure."

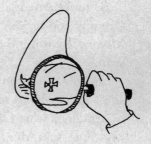

The captain's jaw dropped
in surprise.

"Now that I see it, it makes perfect sense," he said. "As
simple as putting one plus one together. In fact, I think I
recognize the spot . . . it's at . . . wait a minute. I want to
be the one to find it first. Thanks, Meg!"

"I guess you really solved two mysteries at once," Gramps said to Meg a few weeks later. "The Case of the Missing Treasure Map and The Case of the Missing Treasure."

"You amazed even me," Peter admitted. "But I did get some great photos of the whales."

"And look what Captain Quinn gave me for solving the mystery," said Meg. "A whale watch!"

Meg Mackintosh

AND

The Case of the Missing
Babe Ruth Baseball

A Solve-It-Yourself Mystery

by Lucinda Landon

A BANTAM SKYLARK BOOK®
NEW YORK · TORONTO · LONDON · SYDNEY · AUCKLAND

ABOUT THE AUTHOR

Lucinda Landon has been an avid mystery fan since her childhood. In addition to writing and illustrating the mysteries in the Meg Mackintosh series, she illustrated *The Young Detective's Handbook*, by William Vivian Butler.

Ms. Landon lives in Foster, Rhode Island, with her husband and two sons.

RL 3. 007–010

*This edition contains the complete text
of the original hardcover edition.*
NOT ONE WORD HAS BEEN OMITTED.

MEG MACKINTOSH: TWO MYSTERIES
*A Bantam Skylark Book / published by arrangement with
Little, Brown & Company*

PRINTING HISTORY
*MEG MACKINTOSH AND THE CASE OF THE CURIOUS WHALE
WATCH copyright © 1987 by Lucinda Landon. Library of Congress Catalog
Card Number 87-2748
MEG MACKINTOSH AND THE CASE OF THE MISSING BABE RUTH
BASEBALL copyright © 1986 by Lucinda Landon. Library of Congress
Catalog Card Number: 85-20055
Skylark Books is a registered trademark of Bantam Books, a division of
Bantam Doubleday Dell Publishing Group, Inc. Registered in U.S. Patent and
Trademark Office and elsewhere.*

Bantam edition / July 1989

ISBN 0-553-15690-X

Published simultaneously in the United States and Canada

PRINTED IN THE UNITED STATES OF AMERICA

CW   0 9 8 7 6 5 4 3 2 1

For James, Alexander, Eric,
and our grandparents

"Hmm, I do detect a bit of family resemblance," said Meg Mackintosh, as she examined Gramps's old family photo album.

"You've got some funny-looking relatives," remarked Liddy. "And look at these pictures of you and Peter!"

Meg turned another page.

"Gramps, who's this?"

"That's me," explained Gramps, "and that's my cousin Alice. She was always bossing me around. She used to drive me crazy, teasing me about my little dog and calling me 'Georgie Porgie.' I called her 'Tattletale Al' because she was always getting me in trouble.

"I'll never forget the day that photo was taken. We went on a picnic," Gramps reminisced. "That was the day she lost my prize possession."

"What was it?" Meg asked.

"My baseball, signed by the Babe himself."

"A baby signed your baseball?"

"Of course not. Babe Ruth, the greatest baseball player ever. He autographed the ball and gave it to my father and my father gave it to me. I took it to that picnic and Alice lost it. I never saw it again."

Meg examined the photo.

Alice *did* look like a troublemaker. Then Meg spied something else.

The corner of a piece of paper was sticking out from behind the old photograph. Meg pulled it out and carefully unfolded it.

7

August 1928

Dear Georgie Porgie,
Summer is over, it went so fast,
Too bad your poison ivy had to last.
Sorry, I scared you in the hay.
What a pity your kitty ran away.
And the time you hated me most of all,
The day I lost your precious baseball!
Well here's a mystery, here's a clue,
Maybe I can make it up to you.
The answer could be with you right now,
But you wouldn't know it anyhow.

Your cousin
Alice

Clue one
Not a father
Not a gander
Take a look
In her book

"Hear that, Gramps? Maybe your baseball's not lost. Just follow the clue!" exclaimed Meg.

"I doubt it's that simple, Meg-O. Just another of her pranks. I saw that note years ago, but I couldn't make head nor tail of it," Gramps sighed.

"It's probably too old to make sense now," added Liddy.

"But it might really mean something. I've got to investigate," insisted Meg.

Just then the phone rang.

"Hey, Nut-Meg, Peter here. Remind Gramps that I'll be there in the morning."

"Take your time. I've found a mystery. Something to do with a Babe Ruth baseball," Meg teased.

"A Babe Ruth baseball? That's worth a fortune! Don't touch anything until I get there!" shouted Peter.

"Tough luck, Sherlock, I can solve this one myself. Bye."

9

Upstairs in Gramps's boyhood room, where Meg always stayed, she took out her notebook and pencil.

"Finally. The chance I've been waiting for!" Meg told Liddy. "Peter won't let me join his Detective Club until I have 'proof' that I can solve a mystery."

"Well, you'd better do it before he gets here tomorrow," warned Liddy. "He'll never give you a chance."

Meg knew Liddy was right. She sat down at the desk and started a list.

"Take a look in her book." Meg looked at the clue again. "Alice's diary? A nature book about birds?" She gazed up at the shelf of Gramps's old books.

"The Old Woman and the Little Red Hen," Liddy suggested as she squinted at the dusty titles. "Doesn't that fit?"

"I don't think so," said Meg, still jotting in her notebook. Suddenly she reached for a book. "I think I've got it!"

WHICH BOOK DID MEG REACH FOR?

"Not a father, that's mother. Not a gander, that's goose. The Mother Goose book!" Meg explained.

She carefully opened it.

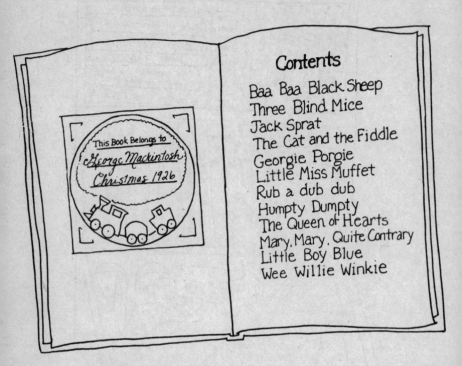

Contents

Baa Baa Black Sheep
Three Blind Mice
Jack Sprat
The Cat and the Fiddle
Georgie Porgie
Little Miss Muffet
Rub a dub dub
Humpty Dumpty
The Queen of Hearts
Mary, Mary, Quite Contrary
Little Boy Blue
Wee Willie Winkie

This Book Belongs to
George Mackintosh
Christmas 1926

"This is definitely Gramps's old book. We must be on the right track," Meg said. After a moment she added, "I think I know where to look."

WHICH RHYME DID MEG TURN TO?

12

"Georgie Porgie, pudding and pie . . ." said Meg.

"Kissed the girls and made them cry . . ." added Liddy as she twirled a pencil in her hair. "So?"

"Georgie Porgie. That's what Alice called Gramps," Meg reminded her. Sure enough there was a small note tucked tightly between the pages. Another clue!

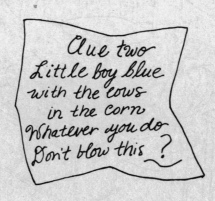

"Little boy blue, come blow your horn," Meg recited.

"But what does a horn have to do with a baseball?" wondered Liddy.

"I don't know yet. First we have to find the horn. Let's see. Foghorn? Cow horn? Horn of plenty? Cape Horn?"

"Well, good luck with it. I have to get home," Liddy said.

Meg walked Liddy downstairs, then went to find Gramps.

"Gramps, did you ever play any musical instrument, like a French horn?"

"No, but I can sing a little. Why?" Gramps replied.

"I found another clue. Alice hid it in your old Mother Goose book, on the Georgie Porgie page. It has something to do with a horn."

"That's easy." Gramps grinned as he pointed to the

bookshelf. Meg followed his finger to the old bugle there. She took it down to inspect it. She removed the mouthpiece, shook it, and peered inside with her flashlight. But no clue.

Gramps got up from the couch. "Well, my dear detective, it's time to turn in. I wouldn't get my hopes up over these clues. Old Alice, she was a sly one."

"Maybe this isn't going to be as easy as I thought," Meg whispered to Skip as they went upstairs to bed.

Meg checked her detective kit. Everything was in order—a magnifying glass, a pair of tweezers to pick up small clues, flashlight and extra batteries, tape measure, scissors, envelopes, and, of course, her detective notebook and pencils.

"I have to be sure to write everything down," she said

to Skip as she got under the covers. "The tiniest fact can solve the biggest mystery. Track, write, decode, deduce . . . then I'll have plenty of proof to show Peter and his Detective Club." After a while she slid her notebook under her pillow and dozed off to sleep.

"Yikes," shrieked Meg. "Stop! Please stop that awful noise!"

Gramps put the bugle down. "If you think that's bad, Meg-O, you should have heard your father play it. I got this bugle for him when he went to Scout Camp. He was a pitiful horn player. Ah well, rise and shine for breakfast."

When Meg got downstairs, Gramps was making pancakes. "All this talk about Alice reminds me of when we were kids. Once she challenged me to a pancake-eating contest. I ate sixteen, while she watched with a miserable grin on her face. When it was her turn, she ate three and forfeited the contest. She had decided from the start to let me win. All I won was a stomachache!" Gramps laughed. "Alice was always getting the best of me."

But Meg was only half listening. She was still puzzled over something Gramps had said earlier. Something had to be wrong with the horn clue.

WHAT WAS IT?

"Wait a minute!" Meg shouted. "Gramps, if you got this bugle for Dad when he was a kid, it *couldn't* be the right horn. It wasn't even *around* when Alice drummed up this whole mystery."

"Guess that's so," Gramps admitted sheepishly.

Meg looked at the clue again. "Whatever you do, don't blow this horn." Remembering another kind of horn, she raced into the living room.

"You wouldn't want to blow this horn, eh, Skip," Meg said as she took the old powder horn off the hook. She pulled off the cap. There was no powder inside, but there was something else. Meg took her tweezers out of her detective kit and slowly pulled out a small, tightly rolled piece of paper.

"I guess I'm not surprised that nobody has looked in there lately," said Gramps. "Maybe you really are onto something, Meg-O. What does it say?"

"I don't know. Does it mean anything to you, Gramps?"

"Never cared much for word puzzles myself," confessed Gramps, "but if you find one of those jigsaw puzzles with the pictures, I'll be glad to help you."

Meg shook her head and sighed. Peter would be arriving soon. She had to solve this mystery fast. Just then the back door slammed and Meg jumped.

"Whew, it's only you," Meg said with a sigh as Liddy came into the room.

"Only me? Only me might help you solve this," Liddy replied as she read the clue. "It looks like a secret-alphabet code. You know, when each letter stands for a different letter in the alphabet."

"Or maybe the letters in each word are just scrambled around," said Meg. She took out her notebook and began trying different combinations.

Before long the door slammed again. Peter was peering over their shoulders.

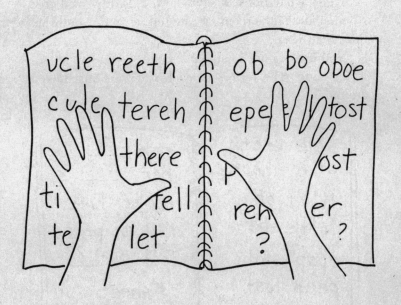

"Here's a clue for you, Nut-Meg, *drop it!*" Peter said. "I can have this solved in no time!"

"I found it, I followed it, and I'll finish it," protested Meg, covering her notes. But not quickly enough.

"What's this? A word puzzle? I could put it on my computer and have it decoded in a flash," Peter persisted. "What's it got to do with a Babe Ruth baseball, anyway?"

Meg snatched the clue back. "Don't bother. I've already figured it out with my own brainpower!"

AND SHE HAD. HAVE YOU?

"Well, what does it say?" asked Liddy, as Peter stomped out of the room. "I counted seven *E*'s, but what does that mean?"

"Nothing. It's not an alphabet code. It *is* a scrambled-letter code. The letters in each word are just mixed around."

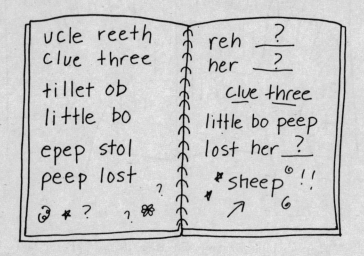

"It says: 'Clue three little bo peep lost her'—her sheep, of course," said Meg.

"Why didn't I see that?" said Liddy, shutting the dictionary.

"Is it something to do with sheep's wool, or an old spinning wheel?" wondered Meg.

"Or a sheepskin?" suggested Liddy.

Meg and Liddy looked high and low. Meanwhile, Peter was eagerly searching the old photo albums, jotting down notes. He was more nerve-racking than Alice and her crazy clues, thought Meg.

It wasn't until later in the afternoon, when Liddy had gone home, that Meg realized what the answer to the sheep clue was.

**DO YOU KNOW WHERE BO PEEP'S
LOST SHEEP CAN BE FOUND?**

"Right in front of me all along," Meg sighed. She carefully unhooked the old painting. On the back, tucked tightly between the canvas and the frame, was another small note. But it had crumbled over time.

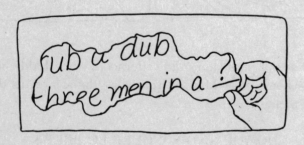

Meg wrote down what she could decipher.

"Aha! Another scrambled code," said Peter, and Meg jumped. She hadn't heard him come up behind her. "Wait until the guys see that baseball!"

"Stay out of this! You don't even know what it's all about," Meg answered. "Anyway, it's Gramps's baseball."

"I think I've got it unjumbled . . . B-U-D-D-H-A!" Peter raced to the statue in the living room.

But Meg knew he was wasting his time. Taking her notes with her, she slipped off to find the answer to the clúe.

**WHAT DID THE CLUE MEAN
AND WHERE DID MEG LOOK?**

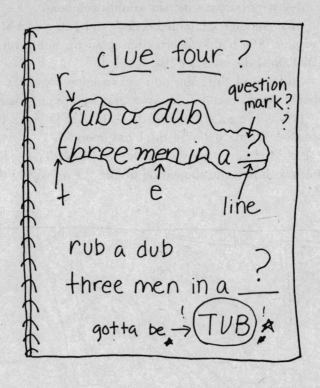

Peter was way off. It wasn't a scrambled-letter code at all. It was a line from another Mother Goose rhyme. Alice must have meant *tub*.

Meg was scouring the bathroom for clues when Gramps leaned in the door. "Sorry to disappoint you, Meg-O, but you won't find much here. You see, it's like the horn. This bathroom isn't as old as those clues."

"A new bathroom? Then where's the old one?" asked Meg.

"Well, we put a bathroom *in* the house, but we didn't take one *out*, so to speak. Back when I was a youngster, we just had an outhouse. We took baths in an old tub in the kitchen," Gramps said.

"This can't be a dead end," sighed Meg. "There's got to be a solution, after I've gotten this far."

"Alice was cunning," Gramps said.

Meg had to agree.

Later that night, Peter knocked on Meg's door. "Are you still sleeping with Gramps's old stuffed animals? A little babyish, don't you think? I gave up that pathetic old dog years ago."

"What do you really want, Peter?" Meg said suspiciously.

"Hey, Meggy, let's put our heads together on this mystery. I could help you out. For instance, the old outhouse, where Gramps keeps his gardening stuff now. I bet that has something to do with it. Well, see ya in the morning, Nut-Meg."

"I'd already thought of that," Meg said to herself, "but I'd better not wait until tomorrow to check it out. Peter might get their first." When she thought that Gramps and Peter were safely asleep, she pulled her raincoat and boots over her pajamas and tiptoed outside. The air was cool and the ground still damp from rain. Meg flicked on her flashlight and headed for the rickety old toolshed.

The flimsy door swung open. Meg spied a pile of tools
and flowerpots and an old rain barrel. Was it an old wash-
tub? It must be—there was a note wedged between the
wooden slats! She pulled it out and opened it up.

clue #4
dig under
the floor

But instead of reaching for the shovel, Meg sat back on her heels and thought. There was something funny about this clue.

HOW DID MEG KNOW?
HINT: THERE ARE FIVE TELLTALE SIGNS.
CAN YOU SPOT THEM ALL?

1. It was on lined paper. All the other clues were on unlined.
2. It was ripped out of a spiral notebook. None of the others were.
3. The handwriting slanted to the left. Alice's slanted to the right.
4. It said "Clue #4"—but Meg had already found the fourth clue.
5. It had nothing to do with Mother Goose rhymes.

Clearly, this was a fake clue. Someone was trying to throw her off the track. Meg was sure she knew who . . .

and after looking around the toolshed again, she knew where.

Someone had been here recently. There were fresh, muddy footprints and the dust marks showed that the cabinet had been emptied. Ten to one, Peter was inside.

Meg picked up the shovel and scraped it around on the floor, pretending to dig. After a moment, she came up with the perfect plan to turn the tables on Peter.

"Yikes!" she said loudly. "Spiders—a whole nest of them! Come on, Skip, let's split!" She slammed the toolshed door behind her, then tiptoed around the side and peered through the window. In a flash, Peter tumbled out of the cabinet and bolted back to the house.

Meg held her breath to keep from laughing. "I'm not scared of spiders," she said to herself, "but you-know-who is . . . Mr. Big-shot Detective! It serves him right for leaving that careless clue."

But, as she headed back to bed, she had to admit she was still no further along in solving the mystery. And time was running out. Mom and Dad would be picking them up the next day at noon.

In the morning, Gramps asked Meg to get some kindling for the wood cookstove. He kept it in a funny-shaped old metal bin. The old bathtub!

Meg searched the old tub for a clue, but there was no note, not a scrap of paper.

"Rats! How else could Alice have left a clue?" wondered Meg as she stirred figure eights in her oatmeal. Gramps always gave her huge spoons. This one had a fancy big *M* engraved on it.

As Meg stared at the spoon, she suddenly had an idea of how a message could have been left.

Just as she suspected, there was something scratched on the bottom of the tub:

"Another clue!" Meg exclaimed. This one looked too authentic to be one of Peter's tricks.

"Gramps, did you have any dogs when you were little?" Meg asked.

"Oh, yes," he replied, "probably a dozen or so. Let's see, there was Nippy and Nicky and Lucky and Flippy and twice as many cats. Gosh, we had a lot of pets—ducks, pigs, ponies, even a parrot."

Then the phone rang. It was Liddy.

"What's happening with the mystery?" she asked.

"Can't talk now," Meg whispered as she noticed Peter at the top of the stairs.

"Is that Lydia-the-Encyclopedia on the phone? Tell her I've got this case just about wrapped up," Peter said as he came down the stairs and glanced over Meg's shoulder. "So what's this latest clue?"

"It has something to do with Little Miss Muffet," Meg teased, "and the spider that sat down beside her, you know, scaring Miss Muffet away!"

"What are you talking about?" said Liddy. "Whatever you do, don't let him get it."

"Don't worry, he's bluffing." Meg hung up. She hoped she was right and that this wasn't all a wild-goose chase. She had some deducing of her own to do—fast. Her only hope was to go back to the beginning.

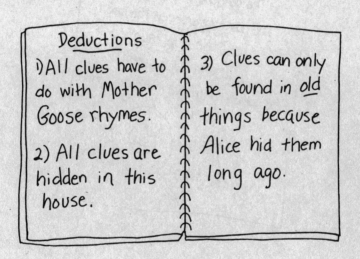

Deductions
1) All clues have to do with Mother Goose rhymes.

2) All clues are hidden in this house.

3) Clues can only be found in old things because Alice hid them long ago.

Meg studied the old clues, then looked at the new one. "'The little dog laughed.' If I'm right, it's part of a Mother Goose rhyme, too. And I think I know which one."

WHICH NURSERY RHYME WAS IT?

Meg found the rhyme in Gramps's Mother Goose book.

The Cat and the Fiddle

Hey, diddle, diddle!
The cat and the fiddle,
The cow jumped over the moon,
The little dog laughed
To see such sport,
And the dish ran away with the spoon.

"This could lead anywhere! Cat, fiddle, cow, moon, dish, or spoon?" Meg tried not to panic. She took out the old photo of Gramps and Alice that had started her on this investigation and reread Alice's letter and clues.

Peter had been upstairs and down, rummaging through all sorts of old stuff. Was he really onto something and she the one off the track?

Meg was determined to solve the mystery. And as she stared at the photo and clue, it all fell into place.

WHAT WAS THE ANSWER?

Meg ran to her bedroom. Safely tucked under the covers was the old stuffed animal that had once belonged to Gramps. The old toy dog. It was the same one that was in the photograph, the one Peter had teased Meg about.

"The little dog laughed," Meg said to herself. "Of course! 'The answer could be with you right now, but you wouldn't know it anyhow' . . . just as Alice said in the letter."

Meg looked at the old toy intently. He was musty and worn. His body was very hard, stuffed with straw.

On his back was a loose thread. It was a different color, as if someone had tried to mend a seam but hadn't done a very good job.

Meg carefully pulled the thread. Sure enough, deep inside the old straw was something you'd never expect to find in an old doggie doll.

The baseball. Just as she had hoped! There was one final note with it, but Meg decided to let Gramps read it.

"What's this?" He woke with a start. "I must be dreaming. My baseball? It couldn't be!"

"It is," said Meg.

"It's what?" Peter burst in.

"It's my Babe Ruth baseball, long lost, and now Meg has found it," Gramps said with a big grin.

"That's right," said Meg. "Alice hid the ball in your old toy dog. With all that hard stuffing, no one ever noticed. She left the Mother Goose clues to help you track it down."

"Amazing," said Gramps.

"Amazing all right," grumbled Peter. "She just got lucky fooling around with those old baby toys."

"Sometimes he reminds me of someone, but I don't know who." Gramps winked at Meg.

"Maybe this will help you remember. It's a note from you-know-who," Meg said, winking back.

Family Album

> August 1928
>
> Dear Georgie Porgie Pudding and Pie,
> This time I really made you cry.
> Your baseball was never lost it's true,
> But I didn't know how to give it back to you.
> I thought a mystery would be fun,
> With some little clues —
> To keep you on the run!
> Your cousin
> Alice
>
> P.S. I hope it doesn't take
> you too long to find it.

"Not *too* long," said Gramps. "Only over fifty years! Wait until I call her and tell her the game is up! And Peter, you be sure to tell everybody back at the Detective Club how Meg-O the supersleuth cracked the case."

Peter groaned. "Oh, all right." Then he even smiled a little.

They heard Mom and Dad's car pull into the driveway. "And solved not a moment too soon," Meg said as she hugged Gramps good-bye.

"You'd better take this along for 'proof,'" Gramps replied, tossing her the baseball.

"Did you catch that, Peter?" Meg laughed. "Wait till the Detective Club sees this!"

Are you ready to read
MEG MACKINTOSH AND THE CASE OF
THE CURIOUS WHALE WATCH?

Just flip the book over to begin.

Are you ready to read
MEG MACKINTOSH AND THE CASE OF
THE MISSING BABE RUTH BASEBALL?

Just flip the book over to begin.